D0514438

This book is published by The Children's Trust to help children with acquired brain injury and their families.

The Children's Trust is the UK's leading charity for children with acquired brain injury, multiple disabilities and complex health needs.

For more information about The Children's Trust, visit www.thechildrenstrust.org.uk
You can find out more about childhood brain injury and visit our parents' forum at www.braininjuryhub.co.uk

There is a guide for grown-ups to accompany this book. Email thehub@thechildrenstrust.org.uk

Thank you to the clinical team at The Children's Trust for their time and expertise in overseeing this book.

For Jenny

Heads Up, TiM-TRON

Ian Ray and Garry Parsons

The
Children's Trust
For children with brain injury

Tim-Tron is a young robot just like any other.

He lives with his family in a little house in **TRANSISTOR AVENUE**

He's usually quite well behaved, but not always.
Tim-Tron loves to play **tricks** on his little sister **Betty-Bot**...

. . . but his mum doesn't always see the **funny** side to his pranks.

*If I've told you once, I've told you a **thousand** times – don't be mean to your sister!*

But Tim-Tron has computed that his mum has actually said this **three thousand times!** He doesn't think it would be a good idea to tell her this, though . . .

At school, Tim-Tron downloads
all of the day's lessons.
He loves racing around with
his friends during games.

Tim-Tron wants to
be a professional
football player
when he's older.

He's in goal today. But as he *dives* to make a **daring** save . . .

cladaaang!

He **bangs** his head
on the goal post!

Tim-Tron has to stay at home to rest after the accident.

"It's **soooooo booooo**ring here, and I miss my friends," he says. "Don't worry, you'll soon be back at school and complaining about it again," Mum promises.

Tim-Tron is back at school, but things have changed in the week he was away. His friends are still talking about football, but he gets **muddled** up with the conversation.

Other things are different, too . . .

Tim-Tron's favourite dinner droid at the canteen has left.

Tim-Tron has been replaced as captain of the football team by Cyber-Simon.

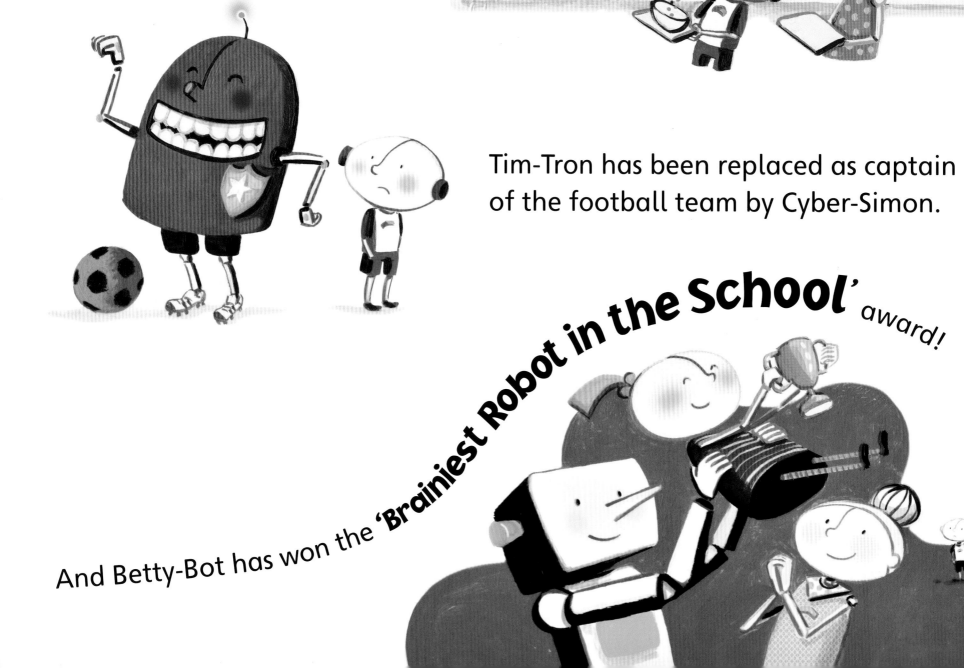

And Betty-Bot has won the '**Brainiest Robot in the School**' award!

But the worst thing is that he feels really tired all the time. His battery level says he's running out of power quicker than before, and it takes longer to download his lessons. This makes Tim-Tron feel grumpy.

We'll have to see the doctor, darling.

Now Tim-Tron feels even more grumpy . . . he *hates* being **prodded** and **poked** at the doctor's!

At the doctor's, Tim-Tron explains
how he **bumped** his head.

*Let's try to find out
what's going on . . .*

"Keep very still," says the doctor. "It won't hurt a bit!"
Tim-Tron stays as still as he can as the bed moves
slowly into a **dark, noisy tunnel.**

The doctor is right and Tim-Tron doesn't feel a thing.

"One of your circuit boards stopped working when you hit your head," the doctor says after the scan.

"This is why your power levels are so low."

"Your other circuit boards are working harder than usual to keep up. So some things are taking you longer to do. We can't fix the circuit board, but there are things you can do to help," he says.

When you get too tired, try to take a break.

Tim-Tron spots Robo-Rita in the waiting room. She has trouble with her **wheels**.

He also sees Otto-Matic, whose **claW** isn't working very well.

"I suppose I'm similar to these poorly robots," he says to his mum, "it's just that my injury is harder to see."

Back at home in Transistor Avenue,
Tim-Tron works out a 'routine'.
This means doing things at
the same time each day.
He powers **up** at the
same time each
morning . . .

. . . and powers **down** at the same time each night.

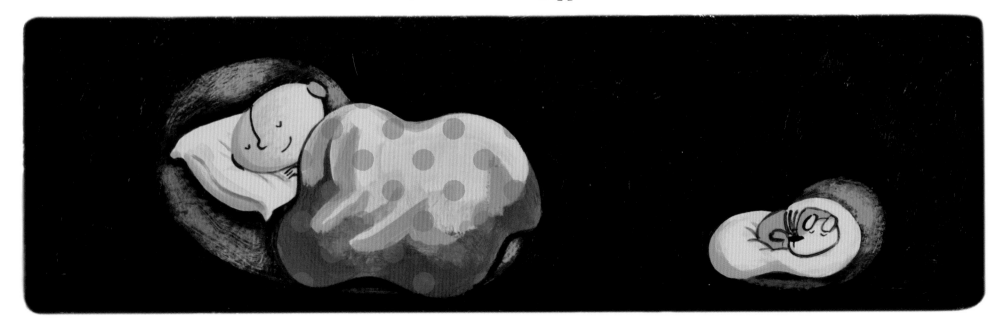

Tim-Tron is feeling much better, so he decides to build his sister a robot cat as a new friend. It's easier to do things in steps, so he writes a plan of things he needs to do.

"I **love** my new friend!" says Betty-Bot.

At school, Tim-Tron speaks to his teacher
about everything the doctor said.
Together, they give the class a special lesson
all about Tim-Tron's circuit board.

This makes Tim-Tron feel much better.

The next day, the teacher says to Tim-Tron: "You're doing so well – would you like to go on the school trip to see the mountains of Mars?"

"Yes please!" says Tim-Tron, excitedly. But he feels a little nervous about going somewhere new.

Tim-Tron decides to make a list of things he needs to pack:

His ticket for the **Mars Express rocket ship,**

his **lunch,**

and his **camera.**

He feels less nervous after making his list.

The trip is **brilliant!**

Tim-Tron sees the beautiful **jagged** mountains of **Mars** from the window of the rocket ship.

He sees **deep**, **dark** caves, and **big** red rocks. "I wonder what all the other planets look like," he thinks to himself.

Back on solid ground in Transistor Avenue, things aren't quite back to normal . . . but they are close enough.

Tim-Tron has changed his mind about being a football player. He's decided to become an astronomer instead.

He still has plenty of time for playing **tricks** on **Betty-Bot**, though . . .

. . . and he's computed that
Mum has now told him off
four thousand times!

THE END